Dear Parents,

Welcome to the Scholastic Reader series. We have taken over 80 years of experience with teachers, parents, and children and put it into a program that is designed to match your child's interests and skills.

Level 1—Short sentences and stories made up of words kids can sound out using their phonics skills and words that are important to remember.

Level 2—Longer sentences and stories with words kids need to know and new "big" words that they will want to know.

Level 3—From sentences to paragraphs to longer stories, these books have large "chunks" of text and are made up of a rich vocabulary.

Level 4—First chapter books with more words and fewer pictures.

It is important that children learn to read well enough to succeed in school and beyond. Here are ideas for reading this book with your child:

- Look at the book together. Encourage your child to read the title and make a prediction about the story.
- Read the book together. Encourage your child to sound out words when appropriate. When your child struggles, you can help by providing the word.
- Encourage your child to retell the story. This is a great way to check for comprehension.

Scholastic Readers are designed to support your child's efforts to learn how to read at every age and every stage. Enjoy helping your child learn to read and love to read.

> **—Francie Alexander**
> Chief Education Officer
> Scholastic Education

Liz

Ms. Frizzle

Written by Jeanette Lane with consultation by Joanna Cole
Illustrated by Ted Enik

Based on *The Magic School Bus* books
written by Joanna Cole and illustrated by Bruce Degen.

The author and editor would like to thank Dr. Paula Cushing, Department Chair and Curator of Invertebrate Zoology at the Denver Museum of Nature and Science, for her expert advice in preparing this manuscript.

ISBN-13: 978-0-545-03587-3
ISBN-10: 0-545-03587-2

12 11 10 9 8 7 6 5   9/0 10/0 11/0

Designed by Rick DeMonico

First printing, September 2007   Printed in the U.S.A.

The Magic School Bus®
Gets Caught in a Web

Arnold   Ralphie   Keesha   Phoebe   Carlos   Tim   Wanda Dorothy Ann

Cartwheel
·B·O·O·K·S·®

SCHOLASTIC INC.

New York Toronto London Auckland Sydney
Mexico City New Delhi Hong Kong Buenos Aires

Today we are learning about spiders.
Ms. Frizzle tells us that spiders are not insects.

A SPIDER FAMILY TREE
by Phoebe

Spiders have been around for millions of years. They lived before dinosaurs.

Spiders are not insects. They are more like these animals:

SCORPION

DADDY LONGLEGS

TICK

"How about a trip to learn about spiders?"
our teacher asks.
Before we say anything,
Ms. Frizzle grabs the bus keys.

THE WIDE WORLD OF WEBS
by Carlos

Different spiders make different webs. The webs can look different and they can work in different ways. All webs are used to catch food.

Spiders spin their webs with silk. Silk is thin, but it is strong. It can stretch more than the elastic in your underwear!

"I don't see Charlotte in the garden," says the Friz.
But we see lots of spiders!
There are spiders hanging in trees.
There are spiders hiding by the house.
There are spiders spinning webs in the grass.

WHERE DO SPIDERS LIVE?
by Wanda

Spiders live anywhere!
Some live in the dry
desert. Some spin webs in
trees. Others live in holes
underground.
You are never very far
from a spider.

There are webs hanging everywhere.
And there is a spider in almost every one!
But there is no sign of Charlotte.

SPIDERS HEAR
WITH HAIRS!
by D.A.

Spiders do not have
ears. They hear with tiny
hairs on their legs.
Sounds make the hairs
move. So spiders feel
sounds on their legs.

The spider grabs the bus-moth with its legs.
But then it walks away.
It does not want to eat the bus-moth.

Ms. Frizzle hands out scissors.
We get out of the bus and cut
the bus out of the web.
We are careful not to get stuck.

When the bus is free we climb back in.
We fly out of the shed and back to the
front of the spooky house.
Our bus becomes a bus again.
A lady is at the front door.

CHARLOTTE!

Back at school, we think about Charlotte.
She loves teaching about spiders.
Ms. Frizzle loves teaching about everything!
What will the Friz teach us next?

Not all spiders make webs to catch food!

Some spiders move around and hunt for their food. These spiders include:

WOLF SPIDER

TARANTULA

TRAP-DOOR SPIDER

Daddy longlegs are not spiders!

They have only one body part and only two eyes. Spiders have two body parts — the head-chest and the abdomen — and eight eyes!

The Best Teacher in the World

by Bernice Chardiet and Grace Maccarone

Illustrated by G. Brian Karas

Hello Reader! — Level 3

SCHOLASTIC INC.

Cartwheel
·B·O·O·K·S·®

New York   Toronto   London   Auckland   Sydney

"Good morning, class," Ms. Darcy said.
"Who would like to take this note to
Mrs. Walker?"
Everyone wanted to go.
Ms. Darcy was the best teacher
in the whole world.
She was very pretty.
And she was very smart.

Martin Kafka waved his pencil case
in the air.
Everything came out.
Brenda Wicker nearly fell off her chair.
"I'll go," she said.
Bunny Rabissi raised her hand
as high as she could.
She wiggled her fingers.
"Ooh ooo ooo! Pick me, please."

"Bunny will go this time,"
said Ms. Darcy.
Bunny popped up from her seat.
She stood up straight and tall.
As she passed Brenda,
Bunny felt a little kick
on her ankle.
But she was too happy to care.

Ms. Darcy gave Bunny the note.
It was on a yellow piece of paper.
The paper was folded in half,
but it was not sealed.

Bunny walked across the room.
She heard a whisper.
"Have a carrot, Bunny Rabbit."
Bunny knew it was Raymond.
He always made fun of her name.
Sometimes it made her cry.

But not now.
Bunny was happy and proud.
She was taking a note to Mrs. Walker.
She held her head up high
and wore a big smile on her face
as she left the room.

Bunny closed the door behind her.

Then her smile went away.

Where was Mrs. Walker's classroom?

Bunny didn't know.

Should she go back and ask?

No, she couldn't.

The others would laugh.

Ms. Darcy would think she was a dummy.

Bunny would just have to try herself.

She started to walk down the hall.

Mr. Sherman's class was next door.
Bunny already knew that.
Mr. Sherman's class and Ms. Darcy's class
got together for recess.

Ms. Stone's class was across the hall.
Bunny looked inside.
Everyone was copying
from the chalkboard.

The next door was closed.
Maybe it was Mrs. Walker's room.
Bunny opened the door.
She hoped no one would notice her.

But everyone did.
The teacher was Mrs. Kyle.
"May I help you?" she asked.
The whole class watched.
Bunny's face turned red.
Quickly she closed the door.

Bunny passed room after room.
She did not see Mrs. Walker.
Many of the doors were closed.
But she would not open them.
Not after she had made the mistake
in front of Mrs. Kyle's class.

Bunny walked up and down the hall twice.
She looked in the library.
She looked in the auditorium.
There was no sign of Mrs. Walker's class.

At last she went back
to her own classroom.
The back door was open.
Bunny waited outside
where no one could see her.

Ms. Darcy was reading
about the ugly duckling
that turned into a swan.
It was Bunny's favorite story.
Bunny wished she were inside.
She wished someone else had taken
the note to Mrs. Walker.
Bunny wanted to cry.

By now, the yellow paper was wrinkled.
What did it say?
Bunny knew she should not look.
But she had to.
Bunny read:

Nancy,
Meet me at Pine Street at four o'clock.
Joyce

Bunny put the note in her pocket
and walked back into the room.
"Did Mrs. Walker say anything?"
Ms. Darcy asked.

Bunny lied.
"She said okay."
Ms. Darcy smiled.
"Thank you, Bunny."

Bunny felt bad all afternoon.
She kept thinking about her fib.
She wanted to tell Ms. Darcy the truth.
But she didn't want Ms. Darcy
to think she was a dummy —
and now a liar, too.

Finally, the bell rang.
It was time to go home.
It was Bunny's last chance
to tell the truth,
but the words would not come out.

That night, Bunny could not sleep.
She thought about Ms. Darcy.
Was she still waiting for Mrs. Walker
on Pine Street?

Bunny didn't want to go to school
the next day.
"Your eyes look a bit red," said her mom.
So Bunny stayed home.
Mom took the day off from work.
They played checkers and cards
and Candyville.
It should have been fun.
But it wasn't.
Bunny felt like a fibber and a fake.
Tomorrow she would have to
go to school.

The next morning,
Bunny looked for Ms. Darcy
in the school yard.
"I have to tell you something,"
said Bunny. "I didn't give
your note to Mrs. Walker."
"I know," said Ms. Darcy.
"I saw her in the parking lot
after school. But you were
very brave to tell me."
Ms. Darcy gave Bunny a hug.
"Just promise me one thing,"
she said. "Never be afraid
to ask a question
when there's something
you don't know. All right?"

"Yes," said Bunny.
And she hugged Ms. Darcy back.
Ms. Darcy was the best teacher
in the whole world.
She was very pretty.
And very, VERY smart.

A NOTE TO PARENTS

Reading Aloud with Your Child

Research shows that reading books aloud is the single most valuable support parents can provide in helping children learn to read.

- Be a ham! The more enthusiasm you display, the more your child will enjoy the book.
- Run your finger underneath the words as you read to signal that the print carries the story.
- Leave time for examining the illustrations more closely; encourage your child to find things in the pictures.
- Invite your youngster to join in whenever there's a repeated phrase in the text.
- Link up events in the book with similar events in your child's life.
- If your child asks a question, stop and answer it. The book can be a means to learning more about your child's thoughts.

Listening to Your Child Read Aloud

The support of your attention and praise is absolutely crucial to your child's continuing efforts to learn to read.

- If your child is learning to read and asks for a word, give it immediately so that the meaning of the story is not interrupted. DO NOT ask your child to sound out the word.
- On the other hand, if your child initiates the act of sounding out, don't intervene.
- If your child is reading along and makes what is called a miscue, listen for the sense of the miscue. If the word "road" is substituted for the word "street," for instance, no meaning is lost. Don't stop the reading for a correction.
- If the miscue makes no sense (for example, "horse" for "house"), ask your child to reread the sentence because you're not sure you understand what's just been read.
- Above all else, enjoy your child's growing command of print and make sure you give lots of praise. *You are your child's first teacher—and the most important one. Praise from you is critical for further risk-taking and learning.*

— Priscilla Lynch
Ph.D., New York University
Educational Consultant

For Cindy and Jane
— B.C.

For Bernice and Jordan
— G.M.

For Sue and Bennett
— G.B.K.

Text copyright © 1990 by Grace Maccarone and Bernice Chardiet.
Illustrations copyright © 1990 by G. Brian Karas.
All rights reserved. Published by Scholastic Inc. Produced by Chardiet Unlimited, Inc.
HELLO READER!, CARTWHEEL BOOKS, and the CARTWHEEL BOOKS logo
are registered trademarks of Scholastic Inc.

Library of Congress Cataloging-in-Publication Data is available.

ISBN 0-590-68158-3

12   11   1 2/0

Printed in the U.S.A.   23